This Little Hippo Book
belongs to

_____

_____

Wrigglesworth

Beech
Farm

Walter's
Garage

Heron
Wood
Lake

Look out for these other

LITTLE RED
TRACTOR

stories published by Scholastic

The Day of the Big Surprise

The Day Stan's World Turned Upside Down

The Day of Molehills and Windmills

Scholastic Children's Books,
Commonwealth House, 1-19 New Oxford Street,
London WC1A 1NU, UK
a division of Scholastic Ltd

London ~ New York ~ Toronto ~ Sydney ~ Auckland
Mexico City ~ New Delhi ~ Hong Kong

First published by Little Hippo, an imprint of Scholastic Ltd, 1999

ISBN 0 590 54466 7

Printed in China

LITTLE RED TRACTOR

The Day Auntie Ellie
Went for a Swim

Story by Peter Tye

Based on the original characters and stories
created by Colin Reeder

Little
Hippo

One morning, there was a loud noise above
Little Red Tractor's cab. Five newly-hatched
swallows were screeching loudly. Their parents
flashed in and out of the barn with beaks full of
food for their hungry chicks.

Stan pushed open the barn door, letting in a shaft of warm sunlight.

"My goodness," he said. "What a lovely noise those young swallows are making! But I'm afraid we'll have to leave them, Little Red Tractor. We're going haymaking today."

Stan and Little Red Tractor chugged off to
Middle Field. Stan hooked Little Red Tractor
on to the hay-turning machine.

They needed to turn the hay so that it dried out.
The cows and sheep would eat the hay during the
cold winter months when there was no grass.

For nearly two hours, Little Red Tractor chugged up
and down the meadow, carefully turning the hay.
It was hot work, but at long last, Stan stopped for a
break and switched off Little Red Tractor's engine.
Patch trotted over to the little brook for a drink

of cool water, while Stan sat down beneath an old oak tree. He took a long drink from his bottle of lemonade and watched the swallows swoop and wheel high in the clear blue sky. They were collecting insects to feed their chicks.

Suddenly, Patch heard something and barked loudly.
Stan got up to take a look. The sheep were grazing
quietly nearby, but down by the river, the lambs were
bleating loudly.

"You're right, Patch," said Stan. "Something's upset the lambs. We'd better go and see what all the fuss is about!"

Stan quickly unhooked the hay-turning machine and drove Little Red Tractor at full speed to Riverside Field.

When they got there, Stan, Patch and Little Red Tractor were surprised to find Auntie Ellie, a very large woolly sheep, standing in the middle of the river. She looked very wet and very sorry for herself.

"Auntie Ellie!" cried Stan. "What are you doing?"
Auntie Ellie bleated a very mournful reply. She
was stuck fast in the mud. She had felt very hot
under her thick woolly coat and had gone into the
river to cool down.

Stan scratched his head.

"Well, you're too heavy for me to lift, Auntie
Ellie. That's a fact." said Stan. "This is a job for
Little Red Tractor."

Stan turned Little Red Tractor round and backed up
to the river bank. Then he put his wellies on and
with a thick rope over his shoulder, began to wade
out towards poor Auntie Ellie.

He was almost there, when Patch barked a
warning. Little Red Tractor was rolling backwards
into the river!

"Oh no!" cried Stan. "I forgot to put the hand
brake on!"

Stan scrambled and splashed his way back and
just managed to pull the hand brake on before Little
Red Tractor rolled into the river.

Auntie Ellie gave a mournful, watery bleat as Stan waded towards her for the second time.

"Hold still, old girl," he said. He carefully passed the rope under Auntie Ellie's middle and made a harness behind her front legs.

But as Stan turned to take the other end of the rope back to Little Red Tractor, one of his boots got stuck in the mud. He pulled. He twisted. He wobbled on one leg and then . . .

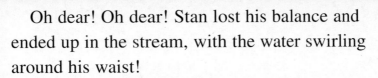

Oh dear! Oh dear! Stan lost his balance and ended up in the stream, with the water swirling around his waist!

"Botheration!" he shouted, as a little silver fish wriggled out from his boot.

The sheep seemed to be grinning at Stan, as he squelched his way to the bank.

"All right," he said to Little Red Tractor, in rather a gruff sort of voice.

"Now let's see if we can get it right this time."
Stan eased the tractor forward. "Gently does it,"
he said. "Slowly, slowly and here she comes!"

Like a great big woolly sponge, Auntie Ellie began
to glide gently towards the bank. The lambs jumped
up and down with excitement, as Auntie Ellie
climbed out of the river.

Stan untied the rope. Then, with water dripping
from her woolly coat, Auntie Ellie ambled up to the
meadow to lie down in the sun to dry.

Stan and Little Red Tractor chugged back to the hayfield.

"Well done, Little Red Tractor," said Stan. "I don't think Auntie Ellie will go swimming again in a hurry!"

Stan and Little Red Tractor got back to work again. Stan chuckled as they drove past his wellies, now gently steaming in the hot sunshine.

"Tell me, Little Red Tractor," he said. "Which do you think will dry first; the hay, my wellies, or Auntie Ellie?"

Stumpy's Mill

Tawny Owl
Wood

Spud
Field

Top Acre

Owl
Wood
Meadow

Middle
Field

Stan's
House

Uphill
Field

Five Oaks
Field

Riverside
Field

Marshy Wood

Downhill
Field

Aunt Ellie's
Willow

Whistling
Bridge

River Rib

Wrigglesworth

Beech
Farm

Walter's
Garage

Heron
Wood
Lake